Speaking Up in Class

CIVIC VIRTUES

Sloane Gould

CIVICS FOR THE REAL WORLD™

Rosen Classroom™

You want to speak in class.

Raise your hand!

Your teacher will call on you.

This makes it fair for everyone.

Everyone can answer questions.

Everyone can read the book out loud.

Everyone can speak up in class!

WORDS TO KNOW

book

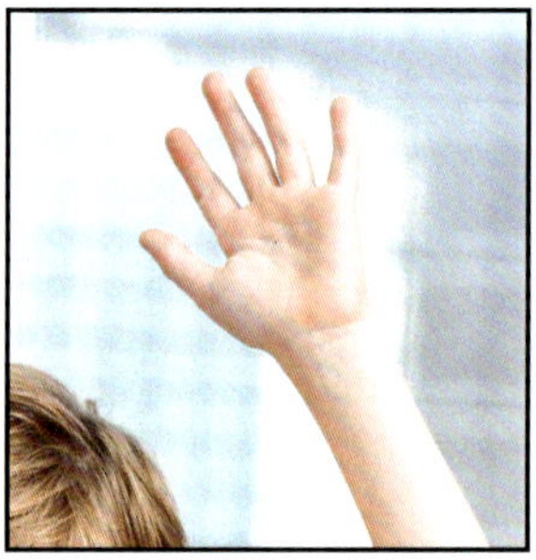

hand

right and wrong ways to raise your hand to speak. Tell students you will all practice raising your hands to speak by playing a game. Explain the game 21 Questions to your class. Tell them that you will think of a word and write it on a piece of paper. Use simple words like bike, tree, or house. Tell them they will each get to ask a question. Example questions might be "Is it a plant?" or "Is it an animal?" or "Is it a machine?" As they try to figure out the mystery word, you will answer yes or no to their questions. Make sure they understand that the entire point of the game is for them to practice raising their hands correctly.

Independent Activity

Hand out a piece of blank drawing paper to your students. Have the students draw a picture of a time when they raised their hands in class. You can also help them write "I raise my hand when I want to speak in class."

Published in 2019 by The Rosen Publishing Group, Inc.
29 East 21st Street, New York, NY 10010

Book Design: Haley Robinson
Editor: Ryan Wolf

Photo Credits: Cover, p. 2, 4, 5, 8 (hand) GagliardImages/Shutterstock.com; p. 3 Sean Locke Photography/Shutterstock.com;p. 6, 8 (book) wavebreakmedia/Shutterstock.com; p. 7 AVAVA/Shutterstock.com.

ISBN: 9781508139355
6-pack ISBN: 9781538363355

Manufactured in the United States of America

CPSIA Compliance Information: Batch #WS18RC: For Further Information contact Rosen Publishing, New York, New York at 1-800-237-9932

CIVICS
FOR THE REAL WORLD™

CIVIC VIRTUES: APPLY CIVIC VIRTUES WHEN PARTICIPATING IN GOVERNMENT, COMMUNITIES, OR SCHOOL SETTINGS.

Rosen Classroom™

9 781508 139355

ISBN: 9781508139355
6-pack ISBN: 9781538363355

B